THE TWELVE DAYS OF WINTER

A School Counting Book

By Deborah Lee Rose
Illustrated by Carey F. Armstrong-Ellis

Abrams Books for Young Readers • New York

1 On the first day of winter,
my teacher gave to me . . .

. . . a bird feeder in a snowy tree.

2

On the second day of winter,
my teacher gave to me
TWO teddy bears
and a bird feeder in a snowy tree.

3 On the third day of winter,
my teacher gave to me
THREE penguins,
two teddy bears,
and a bird feeder in a snowy tree.

Weekly Weather

Monday	snowy
Tuesday	windy
Wednesday	sunny
Thursday	

4 On the fourth day of winter,
my teacher gave to me
FOUR weather words,
three penguins,
two teddy bears,
and a bird feeder
in a snowy tree.

Reminder:

Tomorrow evening—

Skating party!

5 On the fifth day of winter,
my teacher gave to me
FIVE gold stars,
four weather words,
three penguins,
two teddy bears,
and a bird feeder in a snowy tree.

6

On the sixth day of winter,
my teacher gave to me
SIX socks for stuffing,
five gold stars,
four weather words,
three penguins,
two teddy bears,
and a bird feeder
in a snowy tree.

7 On the seventh day of winter,
my teacher gave to me
SEVEN flakes for snipping,
six socks for stuffing,
five gold stars,
four weather words,
three penguins,
two teddy bears,
and a bird feeder in a snowy tree.

8

On the eighth day of winter,
my teacher gave to me
EIGHT bells for jingling,
seven flakes for snipping,
six socks for stuffing,
five gold stars,
four weather words,
three penguins,
two teddy bears,
and a bird feeder in a snowy tree.

On the ninth day of winter,
my teacher gave to me
NINE worms for watching,
eight bells for jingling,
seven flakes for snipping,
six socks for stuffing,
five gold stars,
four weather words,
three penguins,
two teddy bears,
and a bird feeder
in a snowy tree.

10

On the tenth day of winter,
my teacher gave to me
TEN holes for stitching,
nine worms for watching,
eight bells for jingling,
seven flakes for snipping,
six socks for stuffing,
five gold stars,
four weather words,
three penguins,
two teddy bears,
and a bird feeder
in a snowy tree.

snow
snowman
snowball
snowflake
snowstorm
snow peas

11

On the eleventh day of winter,
my teacher gave to me
ELEVEN cubes for gluing,
ten holes for stitching,
nine worms for watching,
eight bells for jingling,
seven flakes for snipping,
six socks for stuffing,
five gold stars,
four weather words,
three penguins,
two teddy bears,
and a bird feeder
in a snowy tree.

12

On the twelfth day of winter,
my teacher gave to me
TWELVE treats for tasting,
eleven cubes for gluing,
ten holes for stitching,
nine worms for watching,
eight bells for jingling,
seven flakes for snipping,
six socks for stuffing . . .

Weekly Weather

Monday	snowy	sleet	miserable
Tuesday	windy	slushy	cabin fever
Wednesday	sunny	freezing rain	
Thursday	cloudy	hail	
Friday	icy	blizzard	

. . . five gold stars,
four weather words,
three penguins,
two teddy bears . . .

. . . and a bird feeder
in a snowy tree.

For all my school experts, big and small, and for Carey,
whose drawings make me want to see more of these characters' adventures —D. L. R.

To the co-op teachers at Coastal Ridge Elementary School —C. F. A-E.

The Library of Congress has cataloged the hardcover edition as follows:
Rose, Deborah Lee.
The twelve days of winter: a school counting book / by Deborah Lee Rose; illustrated by Carey Armstrong-Ellis.
p. cm.
Summary: A cumulative counting verse in which a child lists items pertaining to winter given by the teacher, from twelve
treats for tasting to one bird feeder in a snowy tree.
ISBN 978-0-8109-5472-4
[1. Winter—Fiction. 2. Counting.] I. Armstrong-Ellis, Carey, ill. II. Title.
PzI.R7I49Twe 2006
[E]—dc22
2005011580

Paperback ISBN 978-1-4197-3845-6

Text copyright © 2006 Deborah Lee Rose
Illustrations copyright © 2006, 2019 Carey F. Armstrong-Ellis
Designed by Celina Carvalho and Chad W. Beckerman

Printed and bound in China
10 9 8 7 6 5 4 3 2 1

Abrams Books for Young Readers are available at special discounts when purchased in quantity for premiums
and promotions as well as fundraising or educational use. Special editions can also be created to specification.
For details, contact specialsales@abramsbooks.com or the address below.

Abrams® is a registered trademark of Harry N. Abrams, Inc.

ABRAMS The Art of Books
195 Broadway, New York, NY 10007
abramsbooks.com